AL'S WORLD
SCARED STIFF

BOOK 3

Elise Leonard

ALADDIN PAPERBACKS
NEW YORK LONDON TORONTO SYDNEY

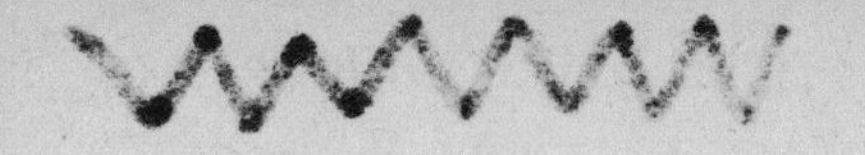

ALADDIN PAPERBACKS
An imprint of Simon & Schuster Children's Publishing Division
1230 Avenue of the Americas, New York, NY 10020

Designed by Christopher Grassi
The text of this book was set in Berkeley Old Style.
Manufactured in the United States of America
First Aladdin Paperbacks edition September 2007
10 9 8 7 6 5 4 3 2 1
Library of Congress Control Number 2006939100
ISBN-13: 978-1-4169-3466-0
ISBN-10: 1-4169-3466-9

ACKNOWLEDGMENTS

This book is dedicated to Aunt Betty, who is ninety-seven years old and still going strong. You're an inspiration! [But John and I did *not* appreciate the time you stopped your car in the middle of a busy intersection and got out (amid heavy traffic) to rub the cramp in your leg. That *wasn't* inspiring! It was terrifying.]

For my wonderful husband John: Even though I give you a *lot* of driving tidbits and advice, you're a pretty good driver. (Except that first time I was in labor. You drove *really* badly that night!)

For my son Michael (who is already driving): If you ever stop your car in the middle of a busy intersection to get out amid heavy traffic to rub a cramp in your leg, you won't have to worry about the other motorists killing you . . . because I'LL kill you!

For my son John (who will be driving next year if I live through teaching Michael how to drive): I'm sorry, honey, but by the time I'm done with your brother, I'll be so freaked out, terrorized, and numb, I'll probably just let you do anything you feel like doing behind the wheel.

For my readers: Hey, guys, thanks for reading AL'S WORLD!!!!

~Elise

CHAPTER 1

I can't believe our parents are letting us do this," I said to Keith.

Keith shrugged. "I guess they figure my grandmother's going to be there as soon as we get off the plane. So how much trouble could we get into?"

I looked at my best friend and smiled.

"Yeah. I know," Keith said. "*You* know and *I* know how much trouble we could get into. But our parents? They have no *clue*!"

"Ladies and gentlemen, this is your captain

speaking. Let's prepare for takeoff," a voice said over the speakers.

With that said, I clicked my seat belt into place.

"Please make sure your tray tables are closed," he added. "And your seats are in the upright position."

"Want some gum?" Keith asked me.

"What kind do you have?" I asked.

"My mom got me a bunch. She got me fruity squares and mint." He took them out of his pocket.

"I'll take a couple of the fruit ones," I said.

Keith laughed. "Too bad," he said.

"Why?" I asked.

"Because I put a couple of vomit-flavored sticks in with the mint. I was hoping you'd take one of those," he said.

Then he started laughing again. He really cracked himself up.

"Let me get this straight," I said. "I'm sitting next to you on a plane. You *know* I get airsick. And you wanted to give me vomit-flavored gum?"

"Yeah," Keith said, laughing. "Wouldn't that have been funny?"

I rolled my eyes. "Not really. You wouldn't have found it too funny when I barfed all over you at takeoff."

He made a face. "Yeah, I guess not," he said.

I rolled my eyes. "Moron," I muttered to myself.

He held out three squares of the fruity gum. Two of the squares were orange. The third was yellow.

"Don't you have any red or purple?" I asked.

"They all taste the same," he said.

"No, they *don't*," I said. "The orange are *orange*, the yellow are *lemon*, the red are *cherry*, and the purple are *grape*."

"Hmm," he said. He looked wowed. "*Really?* I never knew that."

I sighed heavily as the plane's engines whizzed up to speed.

The kid was an idiot. But he had the only gum I was going to get my hands on, so I didn't tell him.

It was tough, but I kept quiet.

"Here's a couple of red ones," he said as he handed them to me. "I know you hate orange-flavored stuff."

I nodded. "Thanks," I said.

"No problem," he answered. "Um, Al?"

"Yeah?"

"Can you do me a favor?" he asked.

"I don't know," I said. "If it has anything to do with your vomit gum, forget it."

"Nah, it doesn't," he said.

"Then what do you want?" I asked.

"Can you hold my hand? While we take off?" he asked.

"*What?*" I looked at him sideways. "Why?"

"Because I get a little scared. And it always helps me when one of my parents holds my hand," he said.

I looked right at him. "I don't know," I said with confusion as I shook my head.

"I won't tell anyone. And it's only during take-off," he said.

His face was getting pale as the engines revved up. It was hard to tell because he's African American and all. But I could tell.

"Please?" he asked.

"I don't know," I said again.

I looked around to see if anyone nearby was watching us. No one even seemed to notice us, which I guess was a good thing. So I rolled my eyes and grabbed his hand. But I also put the flight magazine on top of our locked hands. Just so no one would see.

"Thanks, Al," Keith said.

"Don't mention it," I said. "Ever!"

He closed his eyes, squeezed my hand, and nodded.

"To *anyone*!" I added.

He squeezed my hand and nodded again.

The plane started to take off, and we were now headed for sunny Florida.

I would have been excited about that. *Really* excited. But at the moment, Keith was crushing every *single* bone in my hand.

CHAPTER 2

"A nervous flier, are you, honey?" our flight attendant asked Keith.

She must have come up to the front of the plane as soon as it leveled off.

Keith let go of my hand. Or at least I think he did. I wasn't sure, because it was numb.

I lifted my arm to see what was left of the thing on the end of it. My fingers looked like claws. They were all bent and askew.

It didn't look normal.

"You've deformed me!" I yelled at Keith.

I looked at my claw.

"Maybe a cold can of soda will make it feel better?" our attendant asked with a smile.

"Sure, thanks. And some pretzels, too?" I asked. I showed her my claw so she would feel sorry for me.

"Pretzels, too." She nodded.

"Thanks," I said, pulling my claw back to my body.

"The same for you?" she asked Keith.

"Sure. Thanks. Want some gum?" Keith asked her.

I smacked him in the chest. With my good hand, of course. "Are you *nuts*?"

"What?" Keith asked. "I wasn't going to give her the vomit gum."

"The ol' vomit gum trick, eh?" she asked. She laughed and shook her head as she walked to get us our sodas and snacks. "I wish the airlines would provide that for us to give out," I heard her say.

While I waited for my soda and pretzels, I

looked out the window and saw the clouds below us. "This is pretty cool," I said.

"Can I sit by the window now?" Keith asked. He was leaning so close to me I thought he was going in for a kiss or something.

I pushed his face away from mine. "No. I *told* you. I get airsick."

"Isn't that just when we take off?" he asked.

"No. It's the whole flight."

"Hmm," he said, looking awed. "I never knew that."

"Yeah. Well, now you do," I said.

"Too bad you can't stick your head out the window to get some fresh air. You know, like dogs do," Keith said.

I rolled my eyes. "You idiot. If I stuck my head out the window, two things would happen. First, my head would blow right off. And second, the plane would go down because there'd be a hole in the airplane!" I shook my head. The kid was a complete idiot.

Once again he looked awed. "Cool," he said.

I got angry. "Oh yeah, Keith? Which one is cool? Me sitting here without a *head*? Or the plane going down?"

He started to laugh. "You without a head, of course!"

He looked at me as if *I* were the idiot.

I was just about to hit him when the attendant came back.

"I brought you guys a bunch of stuff. I had it left over from the last flight. It was a much longer flight."

She dumped a whole bunch of little packages in our laps.

There were peanuts, pretzels, cheese crackers, a couple of candy bars, and some granola bars.

"Thanks," I said.

"I've got a couple little boxes of Oreos, too. If you want them," she said.

"Sure," I said. "Thanks! Bring 'em on!"

"I'll be right back." She smiled and left.

She came back with the Oreos a little later.

So there we were. Keith and me. Munching away and looking out the window. We ate like pigs! Then we watched the movie.

Things were going good. Not, you know, *perfect*. But good.

Until I looked out at what was ahead of us.

Straight ahead was a big patch of black.

"That doesn't look good," I said to Keith.

"What doesn't look good?" he asked.

I pointed.

He shoved his big head in front of me to look out the little window.

"No, it doesn't," he agreed.

Once again he started to go pale.

"What do you think it means?" I asked him.

"I don't know." He shrugged. "Maybe it means we're about to die?" he guessed.

I wouldn't have worried too much about it, but we were heading right for it.

"Don't you think we should go the other way?" I asked Keith.

"Yeah. You'd think," he said. "I know *I* would," he added.

I touched the call button above my head. Within moments our attendant showed up.

"Yeah, boys? What can I get for you?" she asked.

I pointed out my window. "What's that?" I asked her.

She pushed us aside and looked out my window.

"That," she said, "would be a hurricane."

She said it simply. Just stating fact.

There was no panic in her voice. No note of pending doom.

She was just telling it like she saw it.

A hurricane.

Great.

And we were headed right for it.

"You think the pilot will go around it?" I asked.

She shrugged. "Depends," was all she said.

"It depends on what?" I asked.

"It depends on who's up in the cockpit," she said.

I could tell she was thinking about it. Trying to remember who was up there today.

I tried to look calm. "So who's driving today?"

She laughed. "No one."

Okay. I was no longer trying to pretend to be calm. "*What?*" I screamed. "There's no *pilot*?"

She laughed. "Of course there's a pilot, silly," she said. "But they don't 'drive,'" she explained.

I couldn't believe my ears. "So what *good* are they?" I demanded to know.

"Yeah!" Keith agreed. "So what *good* are they?"

She had the nerve to laugh. "They don't 'drive' the plane, boys. They *fly* the plane," she said.

She was still laughing.

"Let me get this straight," I said. "We've got some weirdo kamikaze pilot dude who's heading straight into a hurricane. *We're all going to die!* And you're *laughing* at me? Because I said that he *drives* the plane instead of *flies* the plane?"

Okay, so I may have been a bit hysterical right about now.

I guess Keith wasn't the only nervous flier on this airborne death trap.

Just then a man came over the loudspeaker.

"Ladies and gentlemen, may I have your attention, please?"

He paused. Probably to wait for everyone to settle down.

"We've run into a little bit of a problem. A hurricane is hovering right over our landing strip. We have two options," he said.

My mind was wandering. I was thinking of our two options.

Let's see. One was . . . death. The other was . . . well, a *different* type of death.

I wondered which type of death was less painful.

Not that I could have figured it out. Because, well, I didn't know the two different versions. But I knew I wasn't going to be too happy about either one.

This was horrible!

I couldn't believe it.

My life was going to end here. Now.

There were so many things I'd wanted to do with my life.

I wanted to beat Sephiroth in Final Fantasy VII.

I wanted to eat a whole peanut butter and jelly sandwich in one bite.

I wanted to kiss a girl who wasn't related to me.

I wanted to, you know, cure cancer.

CHAPTER 3

Our first choice is to fly around the hurricane," the pilot announced. "We can land at a nearby airport."

People started chattering.

"We have a second choice," he said. "We can fly around up here until the weather moves on."

More chattering.

"So we can circle for a while and see what happens. Or we can land now." He summed it up for us.

Everyone in the plane started talking at once.

"Just remember, folks. We can land. But if we do, we'll all have to find a way to get back to where we were first headed."

I hated to admit it, but he made a lot of sense.

I mean, sure. It was probably better to turn tail and run. That would have been my first choice. Just get the heck out of the hurricane's way.

But he had a good point. We'd all end up having to find our way to where we were headed.

I thought of Keith's grandmother. She was probably sitting at the airport, worried sick about us. And that's not mentioning my mom and dad. Or Keith's parents.

"Do you think the hurricane will, you know, whoosh out of here pretty fast?" I asked our attendant.

She shrugged. "You never know," she said.

"Do we have enough gas to be flying around up here?" Keith asked.

I was surprised. It was a smart question to ask. That's why I was shocked that *Keith* asked it.

She smiled. "We have plenty of fuel. Don't worry about *that*, boys."

I didn't like the way she'd said that. She seemed to indicate that we should worry about *other* things.

That got my mind racing.

"What would *you* do?" Keith asked her.

She laughed. She actually *laughed*!

"I'd stay on board and fly it out," she said.

I looked at Keith.

He shrugged.

"Okay," he said. "That's my vote too."

Keith looked at me. "All right. Whatever," I said. "I'll vote that way too."

Most people agreed. As long as we were safe, we'd stay on board.

That meant circling around until we could land.

All of a sudden the plane was like a party vessel. It was like spring break on wings.

Maybe it was because the adults were buying up those little alcoholic bottles like there was no tomorrow.

I guess they figured if they were going to die, they might as well not feel anything.

Anyhow, whatever the reason, we ended up being one really happy group of people.

After a while the attendant came up to the front of the plane to sit with us.

"You boys doing okay?" she asked.

"Sure," we said.

She handed us a bunch of peanut packets. "Here, take these. Hide them. They're the last of the lot," she said.

Dang. We were out of peanuts? If we didn't land soon, this plane could get *ugly*!

"Folks, it looks like the storm has almost passed through. We should be able to land in about another half hour or so." That was the pilot, talking through the speakers.

People started cheering and shouting. Some were whistling and clapping.

Everyone was happy. Including us. We'd survived a disaster.

It felt great.

The only thing was . . . this wasn't the first disaster of the trip.

And it sure wasn't going to be the last.

At the time, Keith and I had no idea we were headed for a few more.

CHAPTER 4

Finally. Freedom.

We burst out of that plane like racehorses at the starting gate.

"Land," I said happily.

I bent over to kiss the floor of the airport, but some old guy poked my butt with his cane.

"Keep on movin', sonny," he said not-too-sweetly. "I ain't gettin' any younger."

Nice. Real nice.

"Hey, Grams," Keith called to his grandmother, and waved.

She was standing in the lounge area. She looked really worried. "Oh, thank God," she said as she ran to Keith.

She threw herself at him. Almost knocking him over.

He hugged the little old lady and smiled at me over her head. "Grams worries," Keith said. "A *lot*."

She turned around and looked at me.

"Since the day he was born, I had to worry," she said with a wide smile. "He wasn't the sharpest tool in the shed. If you know what I mean," she added.

Yeah. Like *that* was something she had to tell *me*!

"So, you boys are here. Safe and sound. Let's go home now. Okay?" she asked.

"Sure thing, Grams," Keith said.

We went to get our luggage.

Mine came off the plane okay. But Keith's wasn't next to it, so we waited for it to show up.

We waited some more.

When we were the last people standing there, we knew something wasn't right.

A man in an airline jumpsuit passed by. "Um, sir?" I said to him. "My friend here didn't get his luggage."

"That's too bad, boys," he said to us.

We stood there looking at each other.

"So what do we do?" I asked him.

He shrugged. "I guess there's a form or two you'll have to fill out," he said.

So we walked to the airport office.

Then we filled out the stupid forms.

"Don't worry," the little red-haired lady said. "Your suitcase will be found. Just as soon as you leave, probably."

She laughed. But she was the only one laughing.

The three of us didn't find any humor in this. At all.

Once that was done, we headed for the exit doors.

Granny took our hands and led us out of the airport. That's what I've called Keith's grandma for years: Granny.

"Okay, boys. Now the real fun begins," she said cheerfully.

I was hoping so.

So far we almost flew right into a hurricane, and Keith lost his luggage. I'd say for us, this trip was off to a typical start.

And I wasn't too thrilled to be, you know, holding hands. But I figured Granny needed the help walking. So I didn't let go.

Meanwhile, my other hand was going numb from my suitcase.

Oh yeah. The fun was just rushing in now.

When we got to the parking lot, I had to laugh.

"What's so funny?" Granny asked me.

"The cars," I said.

"What about them?" she asked.

"They're all the same," I said.

Keith looked around. Then he laughed too.

"Hey, look at that," he said. "Was there a special sale or something?"

Every car in the lot looked the same.

They were all big and square. And they were mostly light blue.

The ones that weren't light blue were gold. But they were the same type of car as the light blue ones.

It was weird. Really weird.

"How can you tell which one is yours?" I asked Granny.

"Easy," she said. "I wrote down the parking space number."

She let go of our hands and took her little handbag off her shoulder. Then she started digging around in it.

"I can't seem to find the piece of paper I wrote it on," she said softly.

I looked at Keith.

He shrugged.

I looked at the sea of cars. Like I said, they

were mostly light blue. Except for the rare gold one mixed in.

"Let me guess," I said to Granny. "Your car is light blue."

"Yup," she said as she kept digging.

Her pocketbook was tiny. Just like her.

I couldn't see how she could lose anything in there.

"Want me to help you look?" I asked her. I was losing patience.

"No, dearie," she said. "It's in here somewhere."

I looked at Keith and rolled my eyes.

She couldn't find that piece of paper.

"We should just walk up and down the aisles until we find it," she finally said.

So we did.

We walked up and down. Up and down.

Up and down.

By the fifty-seventh aisle I'd had enough.

All the cars looked the same to me. For all we knew, we passed it ten aisles up. Or twenty aisles up. Who knew?

After looking at the one-millionth boxy light blue car, I was done. My feet hurt. My hand was dead. My back was broken. I was starving. And my brain was mush.

But I *did* come up with an idea.

"Does your car have one of those door opener things?" I asked.

"You mean this?" Granny replied. She took out a massive set of keys with the automatic door opener on it.

"Yeah, that," I said.

She offered it to me, and I pressed the unlock button twice.

We heard a car alarm go off. It was way in the distance.

"Could that be your car?" I asked.

She shrugged. "It *could* be."

"You don't know?" Keith asked her.

She shrugged again. "I've been here so long, I can't remember *where* I parked."

We hiked toward the blaring car horn.

All the way back to where we'd started. Well, *almost* where we'd started.

Turns out, her car was in the second aisle from the exit door.

That's one aisle away from where we'd started.

Great.

On the bright side, we'd gotten our *second* disaster out of the way. Third, if you count Keith's luggage.

So as far as I could figure, there couldn't have been any more disasters waiting for us.

Boy, was I wrong!

CHAPTER 5

To say the drive home to Granny's house was "nice" would be a huge lie.

Sure, there were palm trees. That was cool.

And no snow. That was cool too.

But there was also this hot, heavy humidity. It felt like a thick, wet blanket was smothering us. It was hard to breathe.

We passed car after car. Each one had a license plate that read FLORIDA, THE SUNSHINE STATE.

"So, where's the sunshine, Granny?" I asked.

"Wait five minutes," she said.

I was looking around so much that I hadn't noticed her driving.

I started noticing when someone honked at us.

I don't know how I hadn't noticed it. It was awful! Really terrible!

We were weaving in and out of the lane. Like she thought it was bumper cars or something.

"Are you okay?" I asked her.

Keith and I were sitting in the backseat.

"Sure, Al. Why wouldn't I be?" she asked.

"You seem to be weaving a little," I said.

Keith laughed. "Grams always drives like that," he said.

Then, out of nowhere, she just stopped the car.

We weren't at a light. Or at a corner. Or on the side of the road. Just right smack in the middle of the road.

"I've got a cramp," she screamed as she got out of the car.

She bent over and started rubbing her leg. Right there in the middle of the road.

I looked around.

Cars were whooshing by us.

Horns were blaring.

I think I saw some old guy give us the finger.

But Granny didn't notice a thing.

She was bent over. Rubbing her leg. Acting as if we weren't going to get run over by the speeding cars. The ones racing by us at breakneck speeds.

The ones swerving around us. The ones veering like we were a dead animal in the road.

We were going to get killed. I could feel it.

"Get back in the car, Grams," Keith shouted.

I don't know if she heard us. The car horns were blaring loudly as they drove by. She might have missed what Keith said.

"Get back in the car," I repeated. Loudly.

Nothing. No response. Just more rubbing.

And more honking.

And more cars blowing by us.

I swear one almost took her door off.

Did I mention that she left the driver's side door wide open? Because she did.

She finally straightened up. "Ah. That's better," she said as she got back into the big, boxy light blue car.

She shut the door, put the car in gear, and started to drive again.

I looked at Keith.

The poor boy was scared to death. I knew that because he was almost as pale as I was.

"Grams," he said softly.

"Yes, dearie?" she asked simply. As if nothing had just happened. As if we weren't almost killed mere seconds before.

"Please don't do that again," Keith said slowly.

"I had a cramp, dear," she replied. "I can't *drive* if I have a cramp."

She looked at us through the rearview mirror. She was looking at us like we were half-wits.

I heard Keith take a big breath and let it out

slowly. "Then just give us some warning next time. Okay?" he asked.

Yeah, Granny, I thought. *Give us some warning next time so we can jump ship!*

Before we could recover from that little incident, Granny said, "Boys? I have something to tell you."

This didn't sound good. Not good at all.

This morning she didn't feel she "had" to tell us about a hurricane that was headed her way. This afternoon she didn't feel she "had" to tell us where she parked her car. Moments ago she didn't feel she "had" to tell us about a cramp that took her out of the car on a busy highway.

So what could she possibly feel the need to tell us *now*?

I shook my head. This couldn't be good.

I looked at Keith.

He shrugged.

"I have a boyfriend," she confessed.

"So?" I said.

"And?" Keith asked.

"Well," she said, "he's sort of more than a boyfriend."

"What does 'more than a boyfriend' mean?" Keith asked.

The car swerved to the right, even though the road went straight.

An old guy in a light blue boxy car shook his fist out his window. Then he yelled at us. "If you're too old to drive, get off the road!" he hollered.

I looked at him. He had to be at *least* one hundred and fifty if he was a day!

Boy. Talk about the pot calling the kettle black.

"We live together," Granny blurted out.

For a minute there I forgot that we were talking about Granny's boyfriend.

"You'll meet him when we get home," she said to Keith and me.

"Okay," Keith said.

He looked at me. I could tell he wondered what the big deal was. I didn't know. So I shrugged back.

"Please don't tell your parents," Granny begged Keith.

I could tell he thought that was as weird as I did.

I mean, what was she afraid of? That she wasn't old enough?

With that thought, I laughed out loud. But then I realized that it might come off as rude. So I put my hand in front of my face and pretended I had a cough.

Keith looked at me like I was crazy. "What's *your* problem?" he asked.

"Nothing," I said.

Keith shrugged and looked at his grandmother again. "Why can't I tell Mom and Dad?" he asked her.

"Because it's unseemly," she said.

"What's that mean?" Keith asked.

"It's not proper," she explained.

Ya think? I thought.

She answered as if she'd heard me.

"Well, *I* don't think so," she said. "But Keith's parents? They might."

I didn't want to tell her that the thought of two old people living together was totally gross to me.

Plus, she didn't ask me. So I didn't share. But to be honest, I wished *she* hadn't shared.

I looked at Keith. He obviously wished she hadn't shared too.

But I kind of felt sorry for the old gal. I mean, yeah, she was old. But she wasn't dead yet. With that thought, all of a sudden I was on her side.

"Hey," I said to Keith. "It's not like *you* don't keep secrets from your parents," I said in Granny's defense.

"I know," he said. "But what's the big deal? Why can't they know?"

He was asking anyone who would answer.

I sure didn't know the answer to that question. So I let Granny take that one.

"Look, Keith. I just don't need to explain myself to your parents. That's all," she said.

Keith thought about it for a few seconds. "Okay," he answered. "I get it. Fine," he said.

And he really did seem fine with it.

She giggled. "Good. It's our little secret."

Well, it *would* have been our little secret. Except for one minor detail.

When we got home, the geriatric Don Juan was gone.

Missing.

And it didn't look like he'd just gone out for some milk. Or a pack of cigarettes.

It looked like there was a struggle. A big struggle.

The old Romeo had vanished.

CHAPTER 6

The place was trashed. Stuff was everywhere.

The kitchen table was overturned.

Cards were strewn across the kitchen floor.

As I stepped across the tile floor, sugar crunched beneath my feet.

Or maybe it was salt. I didn't know which.

"Oh my God," Granny cried out. "You've got to find him!"

She went running to her living room.

We followed her.

The place was a mess.

The stuffing from the couch was on the outside.

The rocking chair was on its side.

End tables were upside down.

Knickknacks were broken and tossed all over the room.

"Stay here," she said.

She left us in her little living room.

She came back looking scared. Really scared.

Then she turned slowly.

"The bathroom," she said softly as she ran out of the living room again.

I thought she left because she didn't want us to see her cry.

Or perhaps she had to go to the bathroom. We *were* at the airport a long time.

"His medicine. It's still here," she called to us.

She ran into the living room. Then she shook the bottle of medicine in her hand.

"I don't know when he left, but if he doesn't get

this by tomorrow, it's all over!" she said seriously. Dead seriously.

This couldn't be good.

"You boys have to find him," she said.

She didn't look like the cheerful old granny she looked like just a few minutes before.

Her eyes looked wild. Like a caged animal whose cage just got smaller. By half.

"How can we find him?" I asked. "We know nothing about him. Or about this town," I said.

"You *have* to find him," she repeated.

That's all she said. After that she went into this trance that I think was due to shock.

She didn't speak or move or blink.

She just stood there. Holding out his medicine.

Not knowing what to do, I took the bottle from her frozen hand.

I looked at the label. "His name is Earl Simms," I said aloud.

I looked at Granny to see if that got a response

from her. Nope. No response. She was still just standing there.

Keith looked at his grandmother. Then he looked at me. "You think she's okay?" he asked me.

"I don't know," I said. "Do I *look* like a doctor?"

I knew I snapped at him, but I was a little nervous. Granny looked awful.

"Maybe we should put her in a chair," I said.

"Yeah," Keith said. He was still staring at her. "She looks like a tree."

Her arm was still stuck out. As if she were still holding the medicine bottle.

It was creepy.

"You okay?" I asked her.

No response.

"This can't be good," Keith said.

"You *think*?" I snapped back at him.

Great. The person in charge of us was now in a coma. Standing up.

This was freaky.

"Guess we'd better find Earl Simms," I said.

"Yeah," Keith agreed. "But let's see if Grams has anything to eat first."

Good point. We needed to eat before we looked for Earl. "Yeah," I said. "Who knows how long *that'll* take."

We had some ham and cheese sandwiches. And then ate an entire bag of BBQ potato chips. After that we ate the cake that was on her counter.

"What kind do you think it is?" Keith said as he ate his second piece.

"It's some sort of lemon cake," I said. "Can't you taste it?"

He shrugged. "I don't know. It tastes good. That's all I can tell."

I ate a third slice.

"So, what do you think the little black things are?" Keith asked.

"Seeds," I said.

"I figured *that* out," Keith said with a huff. "But what *kind* of seeds?"

I looked at the cake. "I don't know. I think they're poppy seeds."

"I don't like them," Keith said.

"You can't even *taste* them," I countered.

"I know," he said. "But they get stuck in my teeth."

I laughed. "Maybe that's why old people like them."

"Because they get stuck in their teeth?" Keith asked.

"No, because they remind old people that they still *have* teeth!"

"I don't know." Keith shook his head. "You'd think the seeds would get stuck in their dentures or something."

I shrugged. "Your guess is as good as mine. I have no idea why she put the seeds in this cake."

"Maybe when she snaps out of her coma, we can ask her," Keith said. He acted as if his grandmother went into a coma on a regular basis.

"Has she done this before?" I asked.

He shook his head. "Nope. Never."

We walked back into the living room, and she was still standing there. Exactly as we'd left her. Arm sticking out and all.

"Let's see if we can put her in a chair," I said.

We righted the rocking chair. Then we walked her over to it. We pushed her down into the chair.

She was staring straight ahead. Her arm was still sticking out.

"Maybe you should put her arm down," I said to Keith.

"Why should *I* do it?" he asked. He was starting to look pale again.

"Because she's *your* grandmother!" I said.

He looked like he was going to faint.

"Oh, for God's sake," I said as I pushed the old lady's arm down. "There. Was that so hard?"

"I need to get out of here," Keith said. He looked really upset.

"Okay, bud. Let's go look for Earl," I said.

We took Granny's house keys from her purse.

Then we left the house, locking the door behind us.

"You think she'll be okay?" Keith asked.

I shrugged. "I don't know. But something tells me she's not going anywhere."

"That's what I'm afraid of," Keith said.

I knew what he meant. If my grandmother went into a coma, standing up, I'd be a little freaked out too.

"So where do you think we should look?" Keith asked me.

It was raining. But at least it was a warm rain. At home this would be snow.

"I don't know," I said honestly. "What does she like to do?"

"She likes to go to the senior center," Keith said.

"Okay," I said. "Let's start there."

The senior center was just a few blocks away. We got there in about six minutes.

Show tunes were blaring from the speakers placed throughout the center. A peppy tune came on, and I started humming.

By the time we found the main office, I was singing aloud. "The corn is as high as an elephant's eeeeeeeeye," I sang.

Keith hit me in the chest. He knocked the wind out of me. So I couldn't finish the verse.

"This is serious, dude," he said to me.

"I know that, Keith."

"Well, then quit singing!" he yelled.

Okay. So we were both a little stressed out. But I didn't see how my singing was hurting anything.

"How can I help you, boys?" a lady asked from behind the sliding glass windows.

"By any chance, do you know Earl Simms?" I asked her.

"Earl?" she said with a giggle. "Sure, I know Earl. Everyone knows Earl."

Not everyone, I thought. If "everyone" knew Earl, I wouldn't be asking for him, now would I?

And I *thought* I'd made it clear that I had no idea who he was. But maybe I hadn't.

"Is he here?" I asked.

She poked her head out of the glass windows. After she looked around, she said, "No."

That was a big help.

"Do you know where he might be?" Keith asked her.

She nodded.

We waited.

When she didn't say anything, I asked, "Do you think you could *tell* us?"

"Sure, I can tell you," she said with a laugh.

We stood there, waiting.

"Oh," she said with a giggle. "Right."

If she weren't too old for him, I might think this was the *perfect* girl for Keith.

Between the two of them they shared one brain.

CHAPTER 7

He's probably with his best friend," she said with a smile. As if she were proud of herself for knowing the answer.

"And that would be . . . ?" I asked. I moved my hands in a way that showed I wanted more info.

"Luther," she said. "Luther Hail."

She looked at me and smiled.

The woman was driving me crazy. I could deal with one Keith. But two? It was too many.

I took a deep breath and let it out. "And is Luther

Hail *here*?" I asked her. I was gritting my teeth.

She leaned forward and popped her head out of the window again. "No. He's not here."

"Do you know where we could *find* him?" I asked.

"He's probably at home," she said.

That was a big help.

"Do you know where he lives?" Keith asked her.

"Yes," she said.

I stood there and watched these two as they talked together.

It was like watching two monkeys having a chat. It was intriguing and repulsive at the same time. Not to mention frustrating.

When neither said anything next, I lost my cool. "Can you *give* us his *address*?" I shouted.

They both looked at me as if *I* were the idiot.

"Sure. I'll write it down for you, so you don't forget," she said.

She wrote it down and smiled at Keith.

He took it from her hand. "Thanks," Keith said.

I would have asked her for directions to Luther's house. But I didn't have all day to pry them out of her.

We stopped some lady on the street as we left the senior center. She told us how to get there.

Luther lived only a few blocks away, so we got to his house pretty quickly. But by the time we arrived, we were soaked.

He lived in a tiny house. It was more like a cottage.

We knocked on the front door.

"I'm coming," some old guy said.

I assumed that was Luther.

We waited awhile, but he never did answer.

We knocked again.

"I said I was *coming*!" the old coot hollered. "Hold your horses!"

We held our horses.

The old guy finally got to the door.

He swung it open slowly. "I got here as fast as I could," he said angrily. "What do you want? For me to break a hip?" he said with a sneer.

I didn't think answering the front door within twenty minutes was asking too much. And no, I didn't want the old geezer to break a hip.

If he did, then *we* would've had to do something about it.

"So? What do you people want?" he demanded.

Friendly guy, I thought. Yeah, I could see why Earl would choose *this* old codger to be his best friend. Not!

"Do you know where Earl is?" I asked.

"No. Does it look like it's my day to watch him?" he snapped back.

"I don't know," I spat back at him. "*Is* it your day to watch him?"

The old guy was annoying. He had attitude up the wazoo!

"What if it *were*?" he cracked back at me.

"Then I'd have to say you're doing a pretty rotten job of it," I shot back at him.

"Oh my God! Is Earl missing?" Luther asked.

His attitude was now completely gone. In its place was . . . fear.

"Yeah," I said. "It looks like he is."

The old guy nodded. His chins flapped like three flags in the breeze. "We have to get him. Before they kill him."

Okay. This was starting to sound like something I didn't want to get involved in.

I turned to leave.

"Where are you going?" Keith asked me.

"I don't want to get involved with this," I said.

Keith blanched. "But . . . but . . . you *have* to," he said.

"Why?" I asked.

"Because of Grams," he said. "Please. Do it for Grams."

I thought about his grandmother sitting like a, well, a tree in her little torn-up house. She'd looked so pathetic. Not to mention so . . . still.

I wondered if finding Earl would make her move again.

I wondered what would happen when she had to go to the bathroom.

Would she get up?

Would she go?

Would she then go back to the chair and sit again?

What if she just went where she was sitting? The thought that Keith and I would possibly have to clean that up made me snap into action.

"Okay," I said boldly. "Let's . . . find . . . Earl!"

The old guy looked pleased. "Let me just put my teeth in and grab my oxygen," he said as he started leaving the room.

I could now see why it took so long to answer the door. The guy walked slower than a bride coming down the aisle.

Keith and I decided to take a seat while we waited for him to come back.

Keith broke the silence. "It's stuffy in here," he said.

"Yeah," I said. "And it stinks. It smells nasty."

"That's the smell of old age, boys," the old man said as he came back into the room.

I was a little embarrassed for saying that out loud. I felt bad that he'd heard. "Why don't you open a window?" I said as I reached for one.

"No!" he screamed. "There's dangerous stuff out there!"

I tried to think what he was referring to. "Like acid rain?" I asked as I lowered my hands from the window.

"No. Like pollen. And dust," he said.

I looked at Keith.

He shrugged.

"It's not good for an old man," the old man said. "I've got breathing problems," he added.

He really hadn't needed to waste his breath telling us that. We probably could have figured it out by the huge tank of oxygen he was dragging behind him.

Oh yeah. We looked cool.

Not to mention . . . very intimidating.

There we were, two soaking-wet kids, and one really old geezer, dragging his tank of oxygen behind him.

Vin Diesel would be shaking in his boots.

"Sorry about not shaving," the old guy said as he stroked his bristly face. "But when you get old, not having to shower or shave is one of the few pleasures left in life."

Okay, I could understand the not shaving part. But for Keith's and my sake, I *do* wish he had showered.

I felt sorry for the guy. But if I didn't, I would have *definitely* said, "You need a shower, dude!"

Luther turned to a Peg-Board. It was filled with keys. "I guess I'll drive," he said.

He took off a set of keys.

They were shaking in his hand so much, they were jingling.

Great.

"Let's take Annabelle," he said.

I had to ask. "Let me guess. She's big and boxy. And light blue."

He chuckled. "That's right, son. How'd you know?" he asked.

"A lucky guess," I said.

We all piled into the car. Me, Keith, Luther, and his oxygen tank.

"So where are we headed?" I asked Luther.

If I *knew* the answer to that question, I probably would've gotten out right then and there. But unfortunately for me, I *didn't* know the answer.

CHAPTER 8

"Hell" probably would have been the best answer to my simple question. We were going to hell and back. At least that's what it felt like.

We ended up driving all over town and never did find Earl.

"This is bad," Luther said. "Very bad."

It wasn't half as bad as the way Luther drove.

If I thought Granny drove like a blind old bat, Luther was even worse.

His hands shook so much, he could barely hold

the steering wheel. But that didn't seem to bother him. Neither did the fact that he was blind in one eye and the other one kept drifting off to the right.

Every time that happened, he'd veer to the left.

I guess he was trying to make up for it.

But we were all over the road and almost got hit many, *many* times.

"Maybe it would be better if you boys drove," he finally admitted.

"We can't," Keith said.

"Yeah," I agreed. "We don't have licenses."

"Neither do I," he said.

"You *don't*?" Keith and I said together.

"Nah," he said. "They took mine away from me. That was about . . . um . . . I'd say it was . . . fifteen years ago. Maybe twenty."

"Okay," I said. "That's it. We're done for the day. Go home, Luther."

"I *was* getting a little winded," he said.

A little winded? The guy's half blind and driving without a license, and all he can say is that he needs to go home because he's a little *winded*?

"Look, Luther," I started. "Why don't you tell us all you know about this? And tomorrow Keith and I will look some more."

"Don't you want me to come?" he asked. He looked hurt.

I felt kind of bad for him. "As great as you are, Luther, we really need to do this undercover," I said.

Yeah. That was a good excuse. We needed to do this undercover.

"That's right, Luther," Keith said. "No one will give us info if *you're* around. But if it's just two kids, they won't be so cautious."

That was a nice thing to say. I guess Keith felt sorry for the old guy too.

Luther nodded. "Yes, maybe you're right."

We were just about to drive into his garage. Really. I thought he was going to drive right *into* his garage.

But then his shaking hands turned the wheel a little.

His driving style was more like "hit or miss" than actual steering.

He almost ripped off the passenger's side mirror.

"Guess I should back up and try again," he said.

I nodded. "I would."

He backed up and tried again. This time he almost ripped off the driver's side mirror.

"Third time's the charm," he said.

"So they say," I agreed.

Third time *was* the charm. Which was a good thing. Because I was holding my breath. And I didn't think I could hold it for much longer.

"What's that?" Keith asked him.

He was pointing to something weird. I'd swear it looked like a giant-size tricycle.

"That's my bike," Luther said.

Keith tried not to laugh. But it wasn't working out too well for him. "*That's* your bike?" he said around bouts of laughter.

"Yes," Luther said proudly. "What *of* it? I'm eighty-three years old! What did you expect? A ten-speed?"

He had a point there.

"Earl has one too," he said slowly, as if he were forming a great idea. "Hey, why don't you bring that one over here tomorrow morning? That way, each of you can have a bike to get around town."

Great. Keith and me. On giant tricycles. *That* would look cool.

But, on the other hand, we didn't have any *other* vehicles available to us.

Great.

I hoped no one from school was down here on vacation. If anyone saw us, I'd have to kill myself.

But we had no other options.

"Okay, Luther. We'll be back here tomorrow morning. At, say, ten or so?"

Luther looked horrified. "I said in the *morning*, Al! By ten o'clock half the *day* is already gone."

"Well, what time were *you* thinking?" I asked.

He shrugged. "Seven?"

Keith looked at me. He was shaking his head.

I knew what he was thinking. This was our *vacation*. He didn't want to get up at the crack of dawn.

Even if his grandmother was in an upright coma. Or her boyfriend was kidnapped by . . . who knows? It was still our vacation!

"Let's split the difference," I said.

"Okay," Luther said slowly.

"So we'll see you at nine thirty," Keith said as he headed for the door.

Luther made a face and shook his head.

I rolled my eyes. "That's eight thirty, Keith," I corrected him.

Keith stopped short. "Oh. Okay, I guess. Eight thirty," Keith said.

He didn't look too happy.

Neither did Luther.

That was the good thing about compromise. *No one* was happy.

When we got home to Granny's house, she was sitting exactly as we'd left her.

"Do you think she moved?" Keith asked.

It didn't look like she had. "No," I said.

We noticed the answering machine was blinking away.

"You'd better listen to your messages, Grams," Keith said.

When he received no response, he turned to me. "Do you think we should listen to her messages?" he asked me.

"One's probably from your mom," I said.

He nodded. "That's true."

He looked over at the still little woman in the rocking chair. "I hope you don't mind, Grams, but we should hear your messages," he said softly.

When she didn't even blink, he pressed the button on her machine.

"Mom? Keith? This is your daughter. And your mother." Keith's mother sounded confused.

It didn't take a rocket scientist to figure out that with Keith, the apple hadn't fallen too far from the tree.

"Is everything all right? I heard about the hurricane and the delayed landing. I hope you made it there okay, boys. I'm worried about you. Please call back. Well, not now. Because you're not there. So you can't call back now. But call back when you get this message. Okay?"

Then she went on and on about how she knew it wasn't okay because we weren't there to say it was okay. But then she said that as soon as we *heard* the message, we should think it was okay.

Like I said. The apple didn't fall too far from the tree.

I often felt sorry for Keith's dad. But he worked a lot, so he wasn't home much. Maybe he worked so much to get away from his wife and son. But I never had the heart to find out.

The machine beeped after Keith's mother's message.

Then an old man came on. "Bertha? Bertha, honey? Are you there? It's me, Earl."

I looked at Granny to see if she was responding.

The only change I saw was that she was now clutching one hand in the other. But besides that, she was still sitting like a, um, sitting tree.

"Those SOBs got me. They want the key. But I'm not giving it to them. They won't kill me, I don't think. Not until they get the key."

The key? I wondered. *What key?*

"I stole one of their cell phones. From the short fat one. Used the ol' bump and swipe." He laughed. "But I've got to get it back to him before he finds out. I just wanted you to know that I'm okay. I wish I had my medicine, but I think I'll be okay for now."

He *thinks* he'll be okay? I don't know if *I'd* take that chance. But I guess he didn't have a choice.

"So, your grandson must be there now," Earl said with excitement. "I wish I were there to meet him," he went on.

What was this? A pleasant chat between two old people? Or a secret kidnap call?

"Well, honey, I'd better go now. Say hi to Keith and his friend Al. Tell them I'm looking forward to meeting them. I don't know when I'll get back. Or even *where* I am. But I think I'm down by the docks, because it smells really fishy here. And you know how I hate the smell of fish." He laughed then. "It's not even fresh fish. It smells like old fish."

In the background I heard a man say, "Hey, old man. Who are you talking to?"

"Just talking to myself," Earl said. "Nobody here but us chickens," he added.

So. Earl was a comedian. Great.

That should keep him living a lot longer.

"Gotta go, Bertha," Earl whispered into the phone. "I hope to get home soon," he said.

"Hey," I heard a guy yell at Earl. "Where'd you get that phone from?"

"It was on the ground," Earl said. "It probably

fell out of your pocket when you were roughing me up."

Then the phone went dead.

They'd roughed him up?

Oh, my God! Poor Earl!

CHAPTER 9

"Maybe we should go find him tonight," I said to Keith. "And not wait until tomorrow morning."

"Yeah," Keith agreed. "He could be dead by then."

"We'd better change our clothes," I said. "We're all wet. And it'll probably get colder now that the sun is down."

"Good point," Keith said.

I changed my clothes.

"Can I borrow some of your clothes?" Keith asked.

"Sure," I said with a shrug. The only problem was, even with the fact that I wear my clothes three sizes too big, they *still* didn't fit Keith.

"Maybe Earl's more your size," I offered.

We looked through the dresser in Granny's room and found Earl's clothes. Sure, they fit Keith better, but . . .

"Dang, you look stupid," I said to Keith as he hooked the white leather belt around his waist.

His lime-green-and-yellow plaid high-water pants did nothing for him. The matching yellow golf shirt was pretty tacky too.

Keith smoothed down his shirt, then adjusted his glasses.

"Hey," he barked. "At least it matches!"

I looked down at my tomato red T-shirt and maroon cargo pants. "What's wrong with *this* outfit?" I demanded.

"It doesn't *match*," he hollered crankily.

My God! It was *true*! The clothes really *did* make the man! Keith was now a moth-eaten, crabby eighty-year-old man! I half expected him to tell me to get a haircut and a job!

But before he could freak me out totally, I said, "Let's eat before we go out. Okay?"

Keith never could turn down an offer to eat. "Sure," he said with a smile. Maybe the clothes made the man, but he was the same ol' Keith deep down. Easy to distract, if you know what I mean.

We found a few good leftovers in Granny's fridge. Then we polished off the rest of the lemon cake.

"Oh, and grab Earl's medicine, would ya?" I told Keith.

Keith grabbed Earl's medicine. It was still sitting exactly where I'd left it earlier. Just like Granny. Neither one had moved a hair.

We went to the garage and found Earl's bicycle. Or should I say *tricycle*.

"You should probably drive this thing while I sit on the handlebars," I said to Keith.

"How come I have to do all the work?" Keith griped.

"Because you're heavier than I am," I said.

"So?" Keith whined.

I explained as if I were talking to a two-year-old. "So, if you go on the handlebars, the tricycle will topple over. You'll fall flat on your face!"

I didn't mention that I also didn't think I had the leg strength to pedal *his* big butt as well as mine. I had enough trouble riding a bike when it was just me. But me *and* Keith's extra weight? There was no *way*!

So off we went on our tricycle.

Once again I found myself hoping no one from school was anywhere near.

As I sat perched on the handlebars, I thought out loud. "You know, I think we should get a pizza," I said.

"Pizza sounds great!" Keith said happily.

"Not for us, you dimwit! As a cover," I said. "Like we're pizza boys."

Keith nodded. "Hmm. Good cover. Pizza boys," he said.

I swore I saw smoke coming from the top of his head. Keith didn't think much. And when he did, it was a *major* project.

We arrived at Luther's. His front walkway was so wide, we easily drove up to his front door.

We pounded on the door and leaned on the doorbell. "Luther, you in there?" I shouted.

Through the tiny window in the door, I saw Luther hobbling over.

"What do you want?" he shouted.

"It's us, Luther. Al and Keith," I said.

"Yeah? So? What do you want?" he shouted again.

"Can we use your bike?" I asked.

I saw the face he made when I asked. It looked as if it were caving in on itself. Or maybe that was just because he didn't have his teeth in. "Now?" he hollered.

"Yes, now, Luther," I said. "And you don't have to scream, we can hear you."

"Sorry," he said loudly. "I don't have my hearing

aid in. I can't hear a thing without it, and tend to shout a lot."

"Okay," I said. "Whatever. Can we borrow your bike?" I asked again.

"What for?" he asked. "It's the middle of the night."

"We want to go look for Earl. We heard a message from him. To Keith's grandmother. We think he's in trouble."

"What did he say in the message?" Luther shouted.

I had no intention of screaming the secret message Earl left for Granny. People could be listening, and I didn't want Earl in any more trouble than he was already in.

"It's not important," I said. "Can we take the bike?"

Luther started to turn away from the door. "Let me get my teeth in. And my hearing aid. Then I'll come with you."

I could see him shuffling away from the door.

At his present rate, we'd still be standing here next week.

"We need to go alone, Luther. Remember? Just us kids? So no one suspects anything?" I shouted, hoping he'd hear me.

I didn't see how he couldn't hear me. Half the *town* heard me! Heck, I was hoping the guys I *didn't* want to know I was coming couldn't hear me.

He turned around and waved his hand at the door. "Yeah, go ahead. Take it," he screamed. "I'm too tired to start wandering around town now anyhow."

"Okay, thanks, Luther," I shouted at the still-closed door.

"Go ahead," he shouted more loudly. He was waving his hand at the door again. "The key to the garage is under the potted plant."

I looked around. "The dead one?" I asked.

"Do you see any other one?" he barked.

"No."

"Then that's the one," he said. "Now get out of here so I can get some sleep!"

He turned toward the back of his house again and started walking.

"I guess if he doesn't get his sleep he gets cranky," Keith said.

"I think he's cranky even when he *does* get his sleep," I said back. "And it's certainly not *beauty* sleep, that's for sure," I added.

"He looks better with his teeth in," Keith remarked.

I looked at my not-so-bright best friend. "*Everyone* looks better with their teeth in!"

Keith nodded. He was thinking about that. "Yeah, I guess," he finally said.

I shook my head and tried not to hit him. "Let's just get Luther's bike," I said. "Okay?"

We got the key and walked to the garage. Keith took Earl's bike, and we started on our way.

We looked like two giant-size babies on our tricycles. All we needed were diapers and giant lollipops to complete the bizarre picture.

God, this was embarrassing!

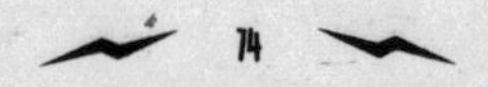

"So, where are we headed?" Keith asked.

"To the docks," I said, pedaling away. Luther's bike was a bit rusty, so it was a little hard to pedal at first. But after a few minutes it got easier.

When we passed by a pizza place, I remembered my thought of using that as a cover.

"Have any money?" I asked Keith.

"Yeah," he said. "My emergency money."

"How much?" I asked.

"Twenty bucks," he said.

I circled my bike around. Wow, did it have a really bad turning radius. On my regular bike at home, I could turn on a dime. With this thing? Forget turning on a dime. I could barely turn on one of those kid-size plastic swimming pools! "These bikes stink!" I muttered.

"Yeah." Keith laughed. "We won't be doing the hitchhiker or a dump truck on these bikes!"

I laughed at the thought. I pictured a hitchhiker. You know, when a rider is rolling with his feet on the front pegs. And he's holding the back tire up so that the handlebars are just skimming the ground.

Then I laughed harder as I pictured a dump truck. Riding on the back wheel, facing backward, with one foot on the peg and the other foot scuffing the tire in the direction you're facing. "Yeah," I said, still laughing. "Guess we won't be doing those!"

Then I really started cracking up. "Or a steamroller, either," I said.

Keith looked at me blankly. "What's a steamroller again? I forget."

"You know," I said to Keith. "When the rider rolls forward with one foot on a front peg and the other foot maintaining balance. Meanwhile, one hand's holding the handlebar and the other hand is holding the seat? With the frame of the bike in front of the rider?"

"Oh yeah," Keith said. "Now I remember." Then he laughed again. "No, I guess we won't be doing any of *those* tricks with these."

We got off our tricycles and moved them close to the door of the pizza place so we could keep an eye on them. Not that I really thought anyone was going to steal our tricycles or anything.

I mean, who were we worried would steal our trikes? A band of rowdy, tattooed old dudes?

CHAPTER 10

We ordered a sausage pizza and waited for it to come out of the oven.

The pizza guy kept looking at Keith as if he were insane.

"Hey," Keith finally snapped. "My luggage got lost at the airport! Okay?"

The pizza guy shrugged.

"I can't fit into my friend's clothes!" Keith continued.

The pizza guy shrugged again and smiled a little.

"These are my grandmother's *boyfriend's* clothes," Keith sputtered. "Not mine!"

The pizza guy shrugged again. "Whatever," he said with that same goofy grin.

"You think I *want* to dress like this?" Keith asked him.

I looked at Keith. "Let it go, buddy. Why do you care what he thinks?"

Keith looked at me and made a face. "Because I think these clothes are turning me into an old man. I feel like I have to teach that young whipper-snapper a lesson!"

"Young whippersnapper?" I repeated. "Keith!" I said with feeling. "That guy's *got* to be at *least* twenty years older than you!"

Keith's face paled. "See what I mean, Al? I'm turning into an old fart!"

He had *that* right. Except for one little point. I felt the need to straighten him out. "Well, to be accurate, you've got to say that you're turning into an old *cranky* fart," I informed him.

Keith looked at me with anger. "Thanks for setting me straight, *pal*," he said loudly.

The pizza man laughed.

"It's so sad to air our dirty laundry like that," Keith said softly. He obviously didn't want the pizza guy to hear us. "Fights like this should be fought in private," he added.

Who *was* this guy? And what did he do with my friend Keith?

I stared at Keith. He looked as if he was going to start crying.

This was *very* strange!

"All right, Keith. Don't worry. Everything's cool," I said. "Okay?"

He sniffled a few times as he nodded. "Okay," he said.

The bell for our pizza rang, and the pizza guy removed it from the oven.

"Pay the man," I said to Keith.

When Keith looked at me with tear-filled eyes, I said, "Please."

Keith nodded, reached down, and ripped the Velcro to open his—I mean Earl's—shoe. Then he took off the white pleather shoe and reached into his black sock.

A black sock? With white shoes? Why hadn't I noticed that before?

Heck, I'd be crying too if I were wearing what Keith was wearing.

He took out a twenty and passed it to the pizza guy.

The guy looked at Keith's folded money and didn't reach to take it.

"Hey," Keith said loudly. "Money's money. Who cares where it came from?"

I felt the need to stick up for my friend. Even if he *was* losing his mind. "Yeah," I added. "You think you know where that money's been *before* he put it in his sock?" I pointed at Keith. "It could've been *anywhere*!"

The pizza guy looked at Keith's banana-yellow-and-lime-green plaid polyester pants. He shrugged and took the money.

We took the pizza.

"So we've decided to hold off our little argument until later?" Keith asked as we left the pizza place.

I couldn't even remember what we were arguing about. "Let's just forget it. Okay?" I asked with a heavy sigh.

"Okay," he said.

As we were walking to our bikes, I said, "I can't believe you wore black socks with that outfit."

Keith shrugged. "I couldn't find any white ones in the drawer. You want to argue over that now?"

"No, Keith." I rolled my eyes. "I don't. I don't want to argue at *all*. About anything."

That finally shut him up.

When we got to our tricycles, we argued over who should hold the pizza.

"I think I should hold it," I said.

"You're *always* the boss of things," Keith harped.

"I am not," I said.

"You are too," he countered.

"Am not," I said more strongly.

"Are too!" he insisted.

I rolled my eyes. "This is stupid," I said.

"Why?" Keith asked. "Because *I* want to be in charge of the pizza?"

We were staring each other down. We looked like two mangy junkyard dogs ready to rip each other's throats out.

Well, *one* mangy junkyard dog. The other was some elderly-looking, rabies-infected dog that had strange, Floridian taste.

"*I* have a basket," Keith said, as if that would make him win.

I looked over at his white wicker basket. It had purple, blue, and green plastic daisies stuck to the front. I guess that was the *macho* tricycle basket.

I rolled my eyes. "Okay, Keith. Go ahead. You can hold the pizza."

He clapped his hands with glee.

Geez. I have *got* to get this kid some cargo or skater pants. Hopefully before he starts shriveling up. Or before his hairline starts receding or something.

We headed toward the water, looking for the docks.

Once at the docks, we rode up and down the roads.

I didn't know about Keith, but I was getting tired.

"I'm hungry," Keith whined.

"No," I said, knowing what was coming next.

"Can I have some of this pizza?" he asked.

"No," I said again.

"Please? It smells so good," he said. I watched as he lowered his head to the box.

"Stay *away* from the pizza, Keith," I said sternly.

"But . . . ," he complained.

"Quit your harping, Keith. First you insisted on holding it, and now you want to eat it," I said.

"So?" he asked. "I had a basket and you didn't."

I saw his hand move from the handlebars over to the pizza box. "Get *away* from the pizza, soldier!" I ordered.

That seemed to snap him out of it. Which was

good. Because I really didn't feel like stopping right now.

A few blocks later I watched as his hand inched toward the pizza box again.

"Don't *make* me have to stop this tricycle, young man!" I hollered at him. "I don't want to have to get off this trike and teach you a lesson, Keith!"

"It's just . . . ," Keith wailed, "all this pedaling's made me hungry again."

"Look, Keith," I said. "Just hang on, okay? He's got to be around here somewhere. We've made it all the way here. You can wait a little longer, can't you?"

"I don't know," he said as he almost crashed into the side of a building. His eyes were plastered to the pizza box. Not to where he was going.

"Keep your eyes on the road, Keith. We're almost there. I can feel it."

"Honest?" he asked.

No, you moron, I'm just trying to get you not to eat our cover! "Yeah, I promise," I lied.

"How will we know what building he's in?" Keith asked.

"I don't know," I said. "Let's start with the ones that have lights on."

"That's a *great* idea," Keith said.

We went from building to building, but most of them seemed to be running a business inside. We finally got to one broken-down old building that had strips of light coming from the back. "Now *that* looks like a place where some people would be up to no good," I said.

"You think?" Keith asked.

"Oh yeah," I said as I inched closer to the building.

The paint had worn off long ago. It was now a grayish shade of rust. At one time it must have been a shiny red building. But not anymore. Now it looked like it was ready to fall apart with one good shove. Boards were splintered with age. Holes the size of Volkswagens were everywhere.

I waved my hand around to catch Keith's attention. When I got it, I held my finger to my lip.

Keith nodded as he got off his tricycle with a groan.

I shot Keith a dirty look.

"Sorry," Keith whispered. "But my bones feel tired."

He walked over to me slowly. "Your bones are going to feel *dead* if you don't shut up!" I hissed.

"Can bones feel dead?" Keith asked me.

He had no idea what I was trying to tell him. I was *trying* to tell him to keep it down before the bad guys in the old broken-down warehouse heard him.

"Yeah," a man with a gruff voice said from behind me. "Bones can feel dead."

I could have sworn I felt the cold, hard barrel of a gun sticking into the side of my neck.

"Be careful, Al. He's got a gun!" Keith cried out.

I rolled my eyes. I couldn't help myself. "Yeah, you *dimwit*. I've already figured that out," I replied.

CHAPTER 11

"What do you two clowns want?" the guy with the gun said. He stuck his gun farther in my neck when he said the word "want."

"Pizza delivery," I chimed.

"I didn't order no pizza," he said gruffly.

"I think it's supposed to be 'I didn't order *any* pizza,'" Keith said with a smile.

Great. Now, of all times, he turns into Mrs. Frost. She was our third-grade teacher. And boy, was *she* a stickler for proper grammar.

I heard the gun cock.

"'I didn't order no pizza' is fine," I said. "*Very* intelligent-sounding." I threw Keith a look.

It was supposed to say, *Shut the heck up before I have a big giant hole in my head, you idiot.* But Keith didn't get that.

"No, Al. I think 'I didn't order no pizza' is *not* fine," Keith insisted.

"Does it *matter*?" I screamed at Keith.

"To Mrs. Frost it would," he said.

I knew it! He was acting like Mrs. Frost!

"Would you do us all a favor, please, and *shut . . . up*?" the guy with the gun said to Keith.

"*Thank* you!" I said to the guy with the gun.

"No problem," he said back to me in his gruff voice. He sounded like a smoker.

He took a few steps over to Keith but still held the gun on me.

"What kind is it?" he asked.

"Sausage," I said.

He went to reach for the pizza, but Keith was

faster. "That'll be nine ninety-nine plus tax, sir," Keith said.

The gun stopped pointing at me and started pointing at Keith. "I didn't order a pizza. But now that you're here, all of a sudden I'm hungry," he said.

"I know what you mean," Keith said. "It smells really good, doesn't it?"

Was Keith *kidding*? The guy was holding a gun on us, and Keith was sharing amusing *remarks*?

The guy took the box of pizza out of Keith's basket. "I'll take this, if you don't mind," he said. "You guys can scram now."

My mouth was hanging open as I heard Keith say, "Well, yes, we *do* mind. Either give us the nine ninety-nine plus tax, or give us back our pizza. We need that pizza for something."

"Um, Keith?" I said softly. "I think we don't need it anymore."

I was trying to tell my *stupid* friend that I think we already *found* our bad guys.

"But we need it for *cover*, Al," Keith said.

The man raised his eyebrows and motioned to the back of the building with his gun. "I think you boys better start walking thataway," he said.

"But what about the nine ninety-nine plus tax?" Keith asked.

"Would you *please* shut up?" the guy with the gun and I asked Keith at the same time.

The guy with the gun tapped me on the shoulder as I was walking toward the back of the building. "How do you stand it?" he asked me.

I shrugged. "It's not always easy. Believe me!"

"I believe you," the guy said.

We walked around to the back of the building. There was a big gaping hole, like a boat had plowed right into the building. It appeared that the boat had won and the building had lost.

The hole was covered up with a big piece of plywood. New plywood. That must've been something they'd brought with them.

"I found these two clowns nosing around," the

armed guy with the gruff voice said into the darkness.

"Who are they?" some other guy asked.

He lit a match and I saw his face. But only for a few brief moments. Then the match went out. And all I saw was the red glowing end of a cigarette.

"I don't know," the gruff-voiced guy said.

He hit me on the side of the head with his gun. "Care to *share* that with us?" he asked.

I kept mum.

"Hi. I'm Keith, and this is my friend Al," Keith said all friendly-like.

Was he totally *insane*?

"A pleasure," the man behind the cigarette said. I saw the little red glow get brighter as he inhaled.

"The pleasure is all ours," Keith said.

"No, it's *not*," I said to the gruff-voiced man and cigarette guy. "And would you puh-*lease* SHUT *UP*?" I begged Keith. He was going to get me killed.

"I can kill him if you want," the gunman offered.

"No, that's okay. My luck, he wouldn't die. Then we'd all have to hear his whining," I said.

The guy with the gun nodded. "Yeah. Good point."

"Al!" Keith said. He sounded hurt.

The idiot didn't even know I was trying to save his life, here!

The man put the pizza box on a nearby table. He opened it up and said, "Hey!"

That caught everyone's attention.

"What?" the voice behind the cigarette asked.

"Someone ate a slice of this pizza!" he complained.

I looked at Keith. Then at the bad guy. Then back to Keith. Then back to the bad guy.

"Give me your gun," I said. "I'll shoot him myself."

"No one's shooting anyone yet. Not without my orders," the guy said from behind his cigarette. "Does *everyone* understand?" he asked the guy with the gruff voice.

Just then I heard someone groan. I wasn't sure, but it sounded like an old person groaning. Like Keith had sounded when he was getting off the tricycle.

You remember that groan. The one that got us caught?

"Our sleeping beauty has awoken," the man behind the red glowing ember said. He sounded excited. "He's coming to his breaking point. I can tell. Keep at him," he instructed the gruff-voiced guy.

"Maybe if he thinks we'll hurt these kids, he'll give it up quicker," the gruff-voiced man said.

They must be talking about the "key." On his message to Keith's grandmother, Earl had said that they were after his key.

"I don't know," the man with the gun said. "I don't think so. After spending time with them, he'll probably beg us to shoot them." Then the guy laughed. "Wait. I think I have a better plan," he said with a chuckle.

"What's that?" the man behind the cigarette said blandly.

"Maybe we should put them all together. Five minutes with *that* one," he pointed to Keith with his gun, "and the old guy'll probably tell us what we want to know just to get *away* from the kid."

He had a point.

"Okay," the guy said with a last draw of his cigarette. "I was running out of options anyhow."

He threw the butt on the floor. I knew that because I saw it fly in an arc to the ground. He must have stepped on it, because I didn't see a red glow anymore.

"Do it," said the voice in the darkness. "Put them all together. If the old man doesn't start talking soon, start killing the kids. And start with the skinny Italian one. He's slightly less annoying. Maybe being stuck with the chatty black one will get the old guy to confess sooner."

"Yes, sir," the gruff-voiced gunman said.

"You know where to find me if you need me" was the last thing the head guy said.

CHAPTER 12

We were told, at gunpoint, to walk to the corner.

Once we got there, the gunman turned on a light. It was one of those camping lights run by batteries. I figured there was no electricity in the old building anymore.

We saw an old man lying on the dusty floor. Despite the fact that he was African American, he looked pale. Very pale. Too pale.

I remembered his medicine and felt around in

my pants pocket. Yup. There it was. His medicine.

"What are you going to do to those boys?" he asked the gunman.

"I would have knocked them off. But it'll be more funny watching you get tortured by them," the guy said with a laugh.

I could hear the wheezing sound of Earl's breath. It was very labored.

"What's that supposed to mean?" Earl asked.

The gunman cracked up. "You'll figure it out soon enough, old man."

The gunman tied us up. He tied my wrists behind my back, then attached my ankles to that.

Let's just say, I'd been more comfortable before.

Well, I'd been *less* comfortable too. So I didn't complain.

Keith, on the other hand, didn't mind complaining.

"Let the games begin," the gunman said with a raspy laugh.

"What does that mean?" Earl asked him.

The man laughed again. A hollow, gravelly sound. "You'll find out," he said. Then he looked at Keith one more time before he walked away. "If you gentlemen will excuse me, I think I'll eat my seven-slice pizza now." Then he left the area.

Earl looked confused. "What's a seven-slice pizza? Is that code for something I should know about?"

"Yeah," I said. "It's code for 'Your girlfriend's grandson is an idiot!'"

Earl looked at Keith. "Keith?" Earl asked. "Is that you?"

Keith wiggled closer to Earl. "Yes, Earl. It's me."

Earl laughed sadly. "You know, I *thought* I recognized those clothes."

Keith looked down at his outfit. "Yeah, sorry about that. The airline lost my luggage," he explained.

"And we got wet from the rain while we were out with Luther. We were looking for you," I added.

"So I had to borrow some of your things. Only

because I couldn't fit into Al's," Keith said with a smile.

"Hello, Al," Earl said, as if this were a tea party and not an abduction and double kidnapping.

"Hi, Mr. Simms. Nice to meet you," I said. Okay, so I felt ridiculous. But I didn't know what else to say. What was I supposed to do? Be *rude*?

"Oh, please, call me Earl," he said politely.

I rolled my eyes at the lame conversation. I tried to turn on my other side, but something was sticking into my leg and it hurt. Then I remembered what it was. Earl's medicine.

"I have your medicine," I told Earl.

"Thank goodness," Earl said. "I'm cutting it close," he added.

I shimmied over to Earl. It took awhile, but between the two of us, we managed to get the bottle out of my pants.

I held the bottle behind my back as Earl popped the lid off with his foot.

"Good thing I could never get those darned

childproof caps off, huh?" he said with a laugh. Either he was delirious or he was very happy to get his medicine. Maybe he was both.

"Yeah," I said as I spilled a couple out on the floor.

Earl leaned down to lick one up. "Oh my God," he said.

"What?" I said, trying to spin around to see what was wrong. "Did you take more than one?" I asked.

Great. It would be my fault that he died of an overdose. I had no idea what the pills were for. But I *did* know that hearing the words "Oh my God" while he was taking them wasn't good.

"The, the, the . . ." Earl was trying to say something, but he was convulsing or something.

"Oh my God!" Keith said.

I looked at Keith. Keith wasn't looking at me. Instead, he was looking where Earl was looking.

I looked where *they* were looking. And then it hit me.

Earl wasn't convulsing. He was terrified. So was Keith.

And now . . . so was I. "Oh my God!" I said as I looked where the two of them were looking.

We were looking at the other side of the building. The building that was quickly becoming engulfed in flames.

"The cigarette," I said out loud. "The guy with the cigarette," I repeated.

"He must've started the fire," Keith said.

Earl looked worried. "This place is old and dry. It's going to burn down in no time," he said.

"What are we going to do?" Keith asked me.

Why did he always think *I* had all the answers? "I don't know, Keith! Do I *look* like I know?" I hissed at him.

"Now's not a good time to bicker, boys," Earl said. "Now would be a good time to find an answer to this problem."

I was always good at coming up with last-minute answers. You know, like on tests. I could get a C-minus better than anyone else who didn't study. It was a gift I had. One I knew would someday come in handy.

Today was that day.

"Okay," I said. "Let me think a minute, here."

My brain was moving as quickly as the fire was moving. Pretty quickly.

I thought about jumping into the water. Nope. That wouldn't work. Tied up as we were, we'd drown in an instant.

Then I thought about moving closer to the flames. You know, so we could burn off the ropes. The flames were across the room and I could feel their heat all the way over here. So no. That wouldn't work. We'd be melted as quickly as a chocolate bar in a fat lady's hand.

I looked around to see if there was a piece of glass somewhere, but nope. Nothing. Not even a shard.

I thought of trying to loosen the ropes by wiggling, and wiggled my butt off. But nope. Nothing moved. The guy had tied me up pretty tightly.

I was wracking my brain. Trying to find the solution.

It was like one of Mrs. Leonard's math problems. She was my math teacher a couple of years ago. She sure had a way of making word problems sound pretty exciting. But in the end? They were just math problems. And were hard to figure out. But that never stopped me from trying.

Sometimes I even found an answer. Sometimes.

But this wasn't one of the times I wanted to mess up. If I messed up *this* problem, my goose was cooked. Well, my *butt* was cooked. And my arms and my legs. And my back and my front.

And no offense or anything, but I kind of *liked* all those parts.

That reminded me of something Mrs. Leonard always said. *The whole is always greater than the sum of its parts.* Or is it that the sum of the parts is always greater than the whole?

I couldn't remember.

But I latched on to the word "whole."

I latched on and couldn't let go.

After a few seconds of thinking about that, it came to me.

"Okay, guys," I said. "I have an idea."

CHAPTER 13

Look, Earl," I said. "Don't be offended. But I need some of your parts."

"What?" he asked. He looked offended.

"Your parts. I need some of them," I said.

Now he looked nervous. "Which ones?" he asked.

"Your teeth," I said.

"My teeth? Why?" he asked.

"They're false like Luther's, right?" I asked.

"Why, yes. They are," he said. "How did you know?"

"I saw the Denture-Grip in Granny's bathroom," I said.

"How do you know that wasn't for her?" Earl asked, as if there weren't a blazing fire ready to engulf us at any moment.

"Because her teeth are crooked. Yours are straight. Perfectly straight. I could see the light from the lantern bounce off them," I said.

"Hmm," Earl said. "I'll have to ask my dentist to make the next pair less straight."

"Um, guys?" Keith asked. "Can we have this little chat later?" He was looking at the blaze. It was about ten feet closer than it was at the start of our little dental talk.

Without further ado, Earl smiled and then spit out his dentures.

He kicked them over to me.

I grabbed the old man's teeth. I tried not to think of the slimy, warm wetness. Or the germs. Or the bits of food that were probably attached. I mean, the man hadn't brushed his teeth in days.

I started rubbing the porcelain teeth over the rope.

I once met an old man who said he could bite through steel with his false teeth. I wasn't trying to bite through steel. Just rub through rope.

I hoped it worked.

"Turn your backs toward the fire," I said to Keith and Earl.

"But then we won't be able to see it coming," Keith said.

Earl cleared his throat. "That might be a good thing, son."

"Just do it," I said. "I saw it in a Vin Diesel movie. He turned his back away from the fire to save his eyes and nose from the heat and smoke."

"Really?" Earl asked. "That doesn't seem to make much sense," he said.

I didn't need a critic right now. Not *ever*, really. But especially not now. "What are you?" I asked. "Some kind of *scientist* or something?" I said mockingly.

"As a matter of fact, I am," Earl said.

Well, *that* blew me out of the water. Not enough to stop rubbing his teeth across the rope, but enough to be a little taken aback. "Really?" I asked.

"Why would I lie?" Earl asked.

I didn't know the answer to that. "I don't know. Maybe to shut me up?" I asked.

Earl tried to heave his shoulders in a shrug. "Sorry, Al. But I really *am* a scientist."

"Oh," I said. "So maybe you can tell us how much longer we have to live?"

I could hear Keith's gulp all the way over here. "You mean we're gonna *die*?" he wailed.

Earl looked at the flickering flames coming closer and then looked at Keith and me. "Don't panic just yet. But there's a good possibility we will," he said.

"Die?" Keith screamed.

"Yes, Keith. I'm sorry," Earl said sadly.

I was sawing those choppers across that rope as fast as my hands could manage. I was rubbing so quickly that I was sure I would start my *own* fire by making a spark.

Because of my frenzied cutting, the rope finally snapped.

I quickly untied my hands and unwrapped my ankles. Then I moved to Earl and did the same to him.

"What about me?" Keith cried. "I thought I was your best friend in the whole world!" he called out.

"You are, bud!" I said to him as soon as Earl was free. "You *know* I always save the best for last!" I said with a happy grin.

We were going to survive! How cool was *this*?

As soon as the three of us were free, we ran to the doorway and shoved the door open.

Standing on the other side was the gunman with the gruff voice.

He had pizza sauce all over his face.

"Not so fast, guys," he said with an evil laugh.

He looked at all of us one by one.

"Very good. You got out of my binding. Quite clever," he said. His laughter was maniacal, and I could see the fire reflected in his eyes.

"We all have to leave," Earl said. "Or we'll all die."

"Look, old man. If I don't get that key from you, I'm a dead man anyhow," he said to Earl. "Now fork over that key!" he screamed.

The flames were licking at our heels.

You'd never imagine how loud a fire gets until you're actually in one. It's deafening!

Not to mention all the pillars and beams that fall all around you. They make a lot of noise, too.

I looked up just in time to see a huge crossbeam dangling down. It was engulfed in flames. It was ready to drop.

We were all standing right under it.

It would have killed us all.

If I hadn't pushed Earl and Keith out of the way just before it came loose.

It came hurtling down with a huge crash. Right on top of the gruff-voiced gunman.

The beam crushed his body, and he was now aflame. His clothes were on fire, his hair was burning, and his shoes were fuming.

It was totally disgusting, but . . . smoke was rising from him.

"I meant to tell you, buddy. Smoking is *really* bad for your health," I said to him.

"He couldn't have died a more fitting death," Earl said.

"Is he the one who roughed you up?" I asked.

Earl pushed aside his pink-and-red-plaid polyester jacket.

I saw blistering red burn marks all over his arm.

"Why didn't you just give him the key?" Keith asked.

"Yeah, Earl," I said. "There's nothing I can think of that's worth taking *that* kind of torture for."

"Ah," he said softly. "But there is."

Keith looked Earl straight in the eye. "No, there isn't, dude!"

"Before I explain," Earl said, "let's see if we can find that guy's little friend."

"No offense, Earl," I said with a smile. "I just want to get the heck *out* of here!"

"Yeah," Keith agreed. "Me too!"

Earl nodded. "Okay, boys, you go on ahead. I'll see you out there," he said as he turned to find the other guy. The one with the cigarette. The one who'd probably *started* this little five-alarm weenie roast.

Keith and I looked at each other.

"We can't leave him in here by himself," I said to Keith.

"Yeah, I know," he said. "I was *afraid* you'd say that."

We turned around and followed Earl farther into the burning building.

"Where are you, you little weasel?" Earl shouted into the flames.

"I'm over here, under this desk. My leg's caught! Help me!" the cigarette guy said.

"Oh, he's not so tough anymore, is he?" I asked Keith.

"It doesn't seem that he is," Keith answered.

"Should we help him, boys?" Earl asked.

The three of us looked at one another.

"If I recall, he didn't seem to mind if *we* died here tonight. Did he, bud?" I asked Keith.

"Nope," Keith said as he shook his head.

"So what's the verdict, boys?" Earl asked.

"Please. Please, help me," the man pleaded.

"Are you *sure* you're really stuck?" I asked him.

"Yes. Yes, I'm sure," he said. He sounded hopeful.

I looked at Keith and shrugged. "Good. So we'll know where to find you if we need you," I said. Funny, but I think I'd just said the *exact* same thing *he'd* said when *our* lives were in danger.

When Earl was convinced the head guy was truly stuck under the desk, we fled the building.

"Elvis has left the building!" Earl announced as soon as we got outside.

My eyes were tearing and my chest felt heavy

from the smoke, but it was a good joke, so I laughed. "That's funny, Earl," I said.

"What is?" Earl asked.

"Your joke," I said.

"What joke?" he asked.

Fire trucks and police cars were surrounding the building. It was total chaos.

"There's a man inside," Earl told the police. "I don't know his name, but I know he's wanted."

"How could you know that, sir?" an officer asked Earl.

"Because he knows who I am," Earl said simply.

We were sitting at the back entrance to an ambulance when Earl asked to use a cell phone.

"I've got two important calls to make," he said. "One's local. One isn't. Is that okay?" he asked the phone's owner.

The person shrugged. "Sure. Go right ahead, sir. I'm a reporter, so all calls are covered." Then he rushed toward the fire.

Earl laughed. "Youth," he said with a chuckle.

"That young reporter's missing the whole story."

"Yeah." Keith laughed. "He thinks it's just a fire. But it was a triple kidnapping, too."

Earl looked at Keith and laughed again. "Youth," he said while shaking his head. "It's wasted on the young."

I listened as Earl called Granny.

"Bertha? It's me. I'm fine, honey. I promise. And I've kept the key, so please don't worry."

When he ended the call, we looked surprised.

"Um, Earl?" I asked.

"Yes, Al?" he said. He looked distracted as he dialed his second number. That one had a *lot* of digits.

"Did Grams answer the phone?" Keith asked.

"No, son. She didn't. I just left a message so she wouldn't worry."

I looked at Keith. He looked at me.

We needed to tell him.

"You tell him," I said to Keith.

"I can't," he said. "*You* tell him," Keith replied.

Earl looked up at us. "What is it, boys?"

"There's something Keith and I have to tell you. It's about Bertha," I said.

I looked at Keith and made a face.

"What is it?" Earl said as he grabbed me by the shirt. "Is she okay? Did they take her, too?"

"No. No, no, no," I said. "It's nothing like that." I looked at Keith again.

"Just spit it out, Al," Earl said without patience.

"She's, um . . ." I really didn't know how to tell him this.

"She's *what*?" he yelled.

"She's um . . ." There was no way around it. I just had to come out and say it. "She's . . . scared stiff."

"I'll bet she was!" he said.

"No," Keith said plainly. "She's *really* scared stiff. Like a tree."

Keith and I did a pretty good imitation of what Granny looked like. We held out our arms like trees and looked blankly into the distance.

"You mean she's catatonic?" he asked us.

We looked at each other. "We don't know. What does that mean?" I asked.

"Yeah. What's that?" Keith asked.

"You've *seen* it; you should know!" Earl shouted.

"You mean, when a person stiffens up like a tree?" I asked.

"Yes!" Earl shouted as he rose from his seat on the ambulance. "I've got to see her. Now!"

Keith panicked. "Is she okay? Should we not have left her like that to come find you?" he blurted out after the old man.

"No," he said. "I'm thankful you found me. But now I have to show her that I'm okay. That the world is okay," he said as he left.

"That was puzzling," I said to Keith.

"Yeah," Keith said. "What do you think he meant by that?"

I shrugged. "I don't know.

CHAPTER 14

I grabbed a nearby EMT guy. "What's 'catatonic'?" I asked him.

"When people freeze up," he said. "Why?"

I didn't answer him. I had more questions of my own. "Why does it happen?" I asked.

"Well, severe shock does that to people sometimes," he said.

"Can it hurt the person who has it?" I asked him.

"Only if it goes untreated too long," he said.

"How long is too long?" I asked.

"It depends on the person, I guess," the EMT said with a shrug. Then he was called over to help a fireman who came out of the building with bad smoke inhalation.

Since no one was watching us, we snuck away from the scene. They'd told us to wait by the ambulances. But we wanted to see how Granny was.

"How *is* she?" we asked when we burst through the door of her little house.

We'd ridden our little tushies off on our tricycles to get there, so we were a little winded.

She was laughing and crying at the same time. *And* she was hugging Earl like there was no tomorrow.

"Thank God. Thank God. Thank God," was all she kept saying.

"Yeah," Keith said. "Your boyfriend's safe, Grams."

"And so is the key," she said.

Keith gasped. And he looked shocked. "I'd *never* figure you to be a gold digger, Grams!" he said with shame.

"A gold digger!" Granny said. "What would make you *think* that of me?"

"You're so worried about the *key*," Keith said.

"What kind of key do you boys think we're *talking* about?" Earl asked.

We shrugged.

"We figured it was to a safety deposit box. Filled with diamonds or money or bonds or something," Keith said.

Granny and Earl threw their heads back and laughed.

"Youth," they said in unison. "It's wasted on the young," they chorused before laughing again.

Then Earl said, "Boys, I'm sorry to disappoint you. But there are things far more valuable than money and jewels."

That sure got my interest. "Like what?" I asked. Listening real well.

This lesson promised to be better than anything I *ever* learned in school.

"Well," Earl started, and then took out his top teeth.

He pushed his fingernail between two teeth.

"Sorry," he said as he put his teeth back in. "I had some rope caught in there. It was very uncomfortable." He bit down on his chompers a few times. "Yes, that's better," he said to himself.

"Well?" Keith asked.

"Yeah," I said. "We want to know!"

"Know what?" Earl asked us.

"What's better than money and jewels?" I said with impatience.

Earl laughed. "Yes. I know. I was just playing with you boys."

He and Granny laughed.

"Yeah," I said. "We know. Youth is wasted on the young."

Granny and Earl looked at each other and laughed.

"Okay, boys. I'll tell you what's more valuable than money and jewels," he said.

I was thinking gold. Or those bare bonds I heard grown-ups talk about so often. Whatever *they* were. I thought that in a couple of Vin Diesel movies they were after some bare bonds. But I wasn't sure.

"Elvis," some big beefy guy screamed as he burst into Granny's little home. "You *left* the building!"

"Yes, sorry. I had to make sure my Bertha was okay."

"Elvis?" Keith asked Earl. "Your name is *Elvis*?"

Earl nodded.

"So Elvis really *did* leave the building?" I asked.

Earl, or Elvis, or whatever his name was, shrugged. "Yes. Sorry."

"Bummer," I said. "I thought that was a cool joke."

"Sorry," Elvis-Earl said again.

"And how did you get here so fast?" the guy asked Elvis-Earl.

Elvis-Earl shrugged again and winced. "I sort of stole a police car."

The man was so angry he was sputtering. "You

don't 'sort of' steal a police car, Elvis! You just . . . stole . . . a . . . police car!" Boy, he was pretty mad now.

Foam was forming at the corners of his mouth.

"I can't keep going through this, Elvis! We place you in the Witness Protection Program for a *reason*!"

"Oh my God," I said to Elvis-Earl. "What did you do? See a mafia boss rub out a peon? See someone wear cement shoes as he got thrown in the river? Witness a president's assassination attempt? View a hit man's hatchet job?"

Elvis-Earl looked at me and smiled. "You watch *way* too many Vin Diesel movies, Al," he said with a chuckle.

"We've seen them *all*," Keith said. *"Twice."*

"Yes, son," Elvis-Earl said. "I figured."

"Enough!" the man screamed. "You're going away again, Elvis!"

"No, I'm not!" Elvis-Earl said. "Before you rudely interrupted, I was about to tell these kids what the most valuable things in life are."

"Yeah," I said to the guy. Whoever he was.

I looked at Elvis-Earl.

He looked at Granny and smiled warmly.

"Love, honor, and knowledge are the three most valuable things in this world," he said.

"That's *it*?" I bellowed.

I felt gypped! *Royally* gypped!

"In that order," Elvis-Earl said with a smile at Granny.

They locked hands.

"I'm tired of running," he said to the man. "There are very few people left who still know of me now. Most of them are dead and buried."

All of a sudden Elvis-Earl looked old and tired. And sad. Very sad. "Before I join them, I think I deserve a little living of my own. Don't you think?" he asked the man.

The man calmed down with Elvis-Earl's words. "I guess so," he said. "It's your funeral, Elvis. This may not be the last of them, you know."

I wondered. The last of who? Or is it 'whom'?

But most notably, why might it not be the last of them? "Who's after you?" I asked Elvis-Earl.

"While he's still here, I'll explain this one last time," the old man said sadly. He nodded toward the big beefy guy.

The big guy nodded silently and looked around the house before Elvis-Earl spoke. "Go ahead," he said to Elvis-Earl. "It's clear."

"I'll tell you boys. But I do *not* want this to leave this room. And I don't want you ever to mention it again. Because I won't either. Do you agree?" he asked Keith and me.

"Yes," we both said seriously.

The old man nodded. "I'm Earl Simms now. But I used to be Elvis Schleuder. Many, many years ago, in the mid-forties." Earl broke out in a sweat.

He had to stop to wipe his brow.

His hands were shaking and he was breathing with difficulty. As if sharing this secret were a thing so awful, it made it hard for him to breathe.

"I worked with a man who helped develop the

atomic bomb. Also called the atom bomb," he said. "You've heard of it?" he asked us.

"Well, *yeah*!" Keith said. "Who *hasn't*?"

Earl nodded. "Well, during that time, I discovered a formula—a secret key, if you will—that would make an even *more* powerful bomb. One that could wipe out an entire *continent* within milliseconds. Plus, it was more portable, virtually undetectable, and could easily fit inside a suitcase."

"Oh my God!" I said as I finally let out the breath I was holding. "What happened to that . . . key?"

"It's still up here," Earl said, pointing to his forehead.

"Why doesn't anyone else know about this?" Keith asked.

I was surprised. That was a good question.

"When I saw what was going on with the testing site in New Mexico, I knew I couldn't share my findings with anyone. If the bomb they'd developed did *that* amount of harm and damage, *mine* would devastate the world!"

"Yeah," I said. "I bet!"

Earl nodded sadly. "With all the greed and power struggles of man, there was no way my key would be used as a method of forcing peace."

"Is that why you developed it?" I asked.

He nodded again. "Yes. I was foolish and naive. I thought it would help bring good. But I saw it would never do that."

"So what happened?" I asked.

"I burned my findings. I destroyed all my research. I told all my assistants that I was wrong. My theory and my work had been too flawed. I tried to walk away."

"But?" Keith asked.

"Yes," he said sadly. "There was a but. But they wouldn't let me go. They kept searching for me and hunting me down. They wanted my formula. My key."

"It's plain that no one's gotten it yet," I said.

"That's true," Earl said. "But every few years, someone tracks me down. Then they try to pry the key from me."

"With all the torture this man has endured, he should surely be insane by now," the big beefy guy said to Keith and me. "He's one tough old bird!"

"And yet, he's also tender," Granny said with love in her eyes.

"Okay, Earl," the beefy guy said. "I'll let you live your life as you see fit. You obviously haven't done anything stupid yet. So I doubt there'll be anyone out there who can break you."

I noticed the man called him Earl and not Elvis this time.

"Thank you, Matt," Earl said to the beefy man. "I do appreciate that."

The man snapped to attention and saluted Earl. "Keep up the good work, soldier!" he barked at Earl.

Earl nodded.

ONE LAST THING . . .

The rest of the vacation was pretty calm.

Granny was totally better. You couldn't even tell that she'd been like she was.

She was terrified that this would be the time the key got out. She thought that without his medicine, Earl would be too weak to fight the terrorists off.

And the guy with the cigarette *was* a terrorist. Turns out his grandfather was one of Earl's original assistants. But the man who'd worked with Earl back then had gone insane, and then two generations of hateful, evil men were spawned after him.

We all hoped that when the terrorist died, so died the last person who could possibly know who Earl really was.

Oh yeah, and Keith *finally* got his clothes. They came on the last day of our vacation.

The poor kid had to wear Earl's old-man clothes the entire time we were down there.

"I kind of got used to them," Keith said as we sat waiting for the plane to take off.

I made a face. "You *did*?"

"Yeah," he said. "Nothing stuck to that polyester. It was pretty cool! It didn't stain, it didn't wrinkle."

"It didn't *breathe*!" I added.

"Yeah, it *did* get hot sometimes in those clothes," he admitted.

"You sure did *complain* enough about them while you were wearing them!" I reminded him.

"Yeah, but now I sorta miss them," he said.

He reached into his pants pocket and said, "Hey, look! My gum!"

He tried to be cool, and flicked it up to his mouth.

So much for cool. It bounced off his nose and hit the back of the chair in front of him. It landed on the floor with a *ping*.

He unlocked his seat belt and bent over to pick it up.

Then he wiped it on his pants and popped it in his mouth. He snapped the seat belt back in place.

He started gagging just as the plane started revving its engines for takeoff.

"You okay?" I asked Keith.

He spit the gum out. Right on his pants.

They weren't polyester, so the gum stuck.

I looked at him.

He shrugged. "Vomit gum," he said simply.

The plane started taxiing forward.

Before he could ask me (because I *knew* he would), I grabbed his hand for the takeoff.

"Thanks, Al," he said softly as he wiped his tongue with his free hand.

"No problem, bud," I said back to him. It was okay with me that he was afraid.

TAKE A SNEAK PEEK AT WHAT AL AND KEITH ARE UP TO IN THEIR NEXT ADVENTURE:

MONKEY BUSINESS

"Al?"

"Yeah, bud?"

"That isn't you, is it?" Keith sounded really scared.

"No. It's not," I said.

"Are you sure?" he asked.

I guess he was hoping. "Not unless I suddenly grew hair all over my body."

"Yeah," Keith said. "Your arms do look really hairy."

I didn't know how to tell him. "They're not my arms, bud."

I saw Keith stiffen with fear. "Are you sure?" he asked.

"Yup. I'm sure," I said.

"Well, if you don't mind my asking, whose arms *are* they?" he asked with care.

I didn't know how to answer him. Mostly because I didn't believe what I was seeing.

"I think it's a troll, dude," I said to Keith.

"Do you think it comes in peace?" he asked.

"It's a gnome, not an alien, Keith." I rolled my eyes.

"Do you see a bridge nearby?" he asked.

I didn't get why he'd ask such a stupid question. But we were talking about Keith here. Plus, it made me laugh a little. "Why? You want to jump off it?"

"No. I was just wondering if he's far from home," Keith said slowly.

All of a sudden the troll started squealing and jumping up and down. Then it started scratching its underarms. If I hadn't known any better, I'd have sworn it was a monkey.

Then I looked closer. It *was* a monkey. "Hey. It's

a monkey, Keith," I said loudly.

Keith finally turned around. He looked right at the monkey and smiled. "Well, look at that. It *is* a monkey," he said. "Have any bananas, Al?"

"Yeah. I always walk around with bananas on me."

Keith held his hand toward the monkey. "I was only asking. You don't have to get all huffy about it."

I watched as the monkey took Keith's hand. "Hey, look at that! He likes you," I said with wonder. Not that I *didn't* think it would like Keith. I mean, Keith's a likable kind of person. It's just that I'd never had a monkey as a friend before.

"I like him, too," Keith said as he smiled at the monkey.

The monkey started rolling his lips back. He looked like he had on wax lips.

"Hey, he's funny. Isn't he?" Keith asked.

Then the monkey started making loud kissing noises and moving his lips like he wanted to kiss Keith.

"Oh yeah. He's funny, all right!" I said.

The monkey was blowing kisses at Keith and trying to take Keith's glasses off. "He wants your glasses. Give him your glasses," I said to Keith.

"No way! If I break another pair, my parents said I'll have to buy the next pair myself."

The monkey was getting restless. "Well, give him something, Keith. Can't you tell he wants to play?"

Keith handed over his book.

The monkey took it. He looked at it closely, then bit the corner.

I could tell by his face that he wasn't impressed.

He threw the book to the ground and started to jump on it, stomping his weird-looking feet all over it.

"Yeah. I feel the same way about that book," Keith said to the monkey.

The monkey was really getting into it now. He was screaming loudly and making a big racket. I was afraid someone would notice him.

"Hey, Keith. Quiet him down, would you? If someone sees him, he'll be in trouble," I said.

"Or *we'll* be in trouble," Keith added as he got up to get his book back.

As Keith leaned over the book, the monkey jumped on Keith. He was hugging and kissing Keith like crazy.

"He's really into you," I said with a laugh.

"I think he's a she," Keith replied.

"How do you know?" I asked.

"I don't know. It's just a feeling," Keith said. The monkey was smacking his—or her—lips at Keith. It looked like it was blowing kisses at Keith.

I laughed again. "Well then, it looks like you've got a girlfriend there, bud."

Keith rolled his eyes. "Very funny," he said as the monkey kissed him right smack on the lips.

"Or maybe you're married now," I added. "I wouldn't know. I don't speak monkey."

"Come on, Al. This isn't funny."

"It is from over here," I said with a big grin.

The monkey was all over Keith. Hugging and kissing him like there was no tomorrow. Of course, that's when the monkey decided to jump over to me. Right in my arms. Then it started kissing me, too.

I kept my mouth shut and swore I wouldn't open it no matter what!

As the monkey started to pick stuff from my hair, I figured it was safe to speak. "Great," I said.

"Look, Al. She's grooming you. She can't decide who to choose: me or you."

I put my hand over my mouth in case she wanted another smooch. I didn't need monkey germs or anything. "We can't leave her here," I said to Keith from behind my hand. "If someone finds her, they might take her somewhere bad."

"Like where?" Keith asked.

"I don't know! Do I look like I know?" I shouted, forgetting about covering my mouth. It was too late. She planted a big wet one right on me. "Great!" I hollered as I repeatedly spit out all the spit in my mouth. "Just great! Now I'll probably get some rare monkey disease or something!" I muttered to myself. Then I said to Keith, "Look, I have to get my bike to bring it home. So until we can figure out what to do with her, *you'll* have to take her home."

"Why can't she go with you?" Keith asked.

"Because, you moron, I can't take her." Keith could be such an idiot sometimes!

"Why not?" he asked.

"Because it would look stupid driving a bike with a *monkey* on the back," I said. I mean, I had a point. A good point. One I thought was obvious!

"But what if she wants to go with you?" Keith asked.

"Well, it doesn't matter who she *wants*, Keith. She'll *have* to go home with you," I said as I pointed to my bike. "Remember? Monkey on back of bike equals . . . no!"

I got on my bike to make my point when I heard Keith blurt out, "She can't come home with me!"

"Why not?" I asked.

Keith looked at the monkey, and I could've sworn he looked depressed. "Because my mother's allergic," he said sadly.

I looked at him closely. He'd said some stupid things in his day, but this? This was probably the stupidest thing I'd ever heard him say. "Your mother's allergic?" I questioned.

"Yeah," he said.

"To *monkeys*?" I yelled at him.

"Many people have allergies," he said as an excuse.

I could tell he was trying to defend his mother. But really! Allergic to *monkeys*? That was just . . . stupid.

"People are allergic to cats, Keith. Or dogs. Maybe trees. Or grass. But *monkeys*?" I shook my head. "I don't think so!"

"She is, Al. My mom's allergic to monkeys. Really!"

It was hard to believe him.